D0971200

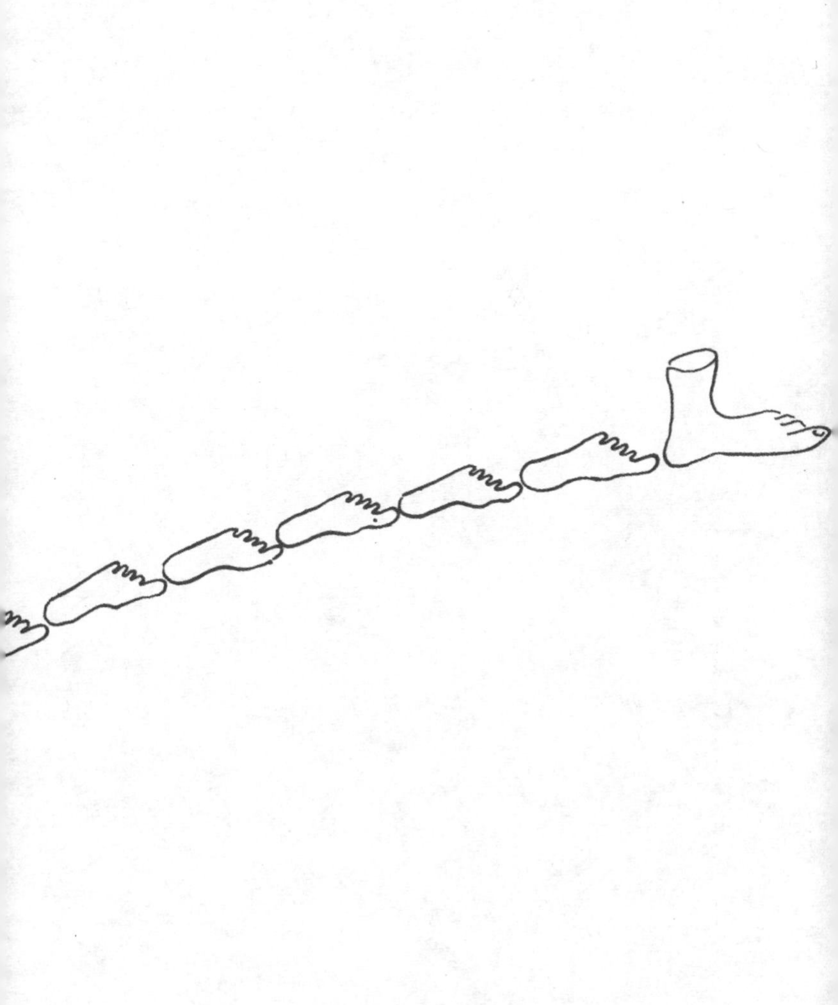

HOW BIG IS A FOOT?

OTHER YEARLING BOOKS YOU WILL ENJOY:

DON'T EAT TOO MUCH TURKEY, *Miriam Cohen*
WHEN WILL I READ?, *Miriam Cohen*
FIRST GRADE TAKES A TEST, *Miriam Cohen*
JIM'S DOG MUFFINS, *Miriam Cohen*
SEE YOU IN SECOND GRADE!, *Miriam Cohen*
STARRING FIRST GRADE, *Miriam Cohen*
LOST IN THE MUSEUM, *Miriam Cohen*
LIAR, LIAR, PANTS ON FIRE!, *Miriam Cohen*
FISH FACE, *Patricia Reilly Giff*
IN THE DINOSAUR'S PAW, *Patricia Reilly Giff*

YEARLING BOOKS are designed especially to entertain and enlighten young people. Patricia Reilly Giff, consultant to this series, received her bachelor's degree from Marymount College and a master's degree in history from St. John's University. She holds a Professional Diploma in Reading and a Doctorate of Humane Letters from Hofstra University. She was a teacher and reading consultant for many years, and is the author of numerous books for young readers.

WRITTEN
AND ILLUSTRATED BY
ROLF MYLLER

HOW BIG IS A

FOOT?

A YOUNG YEARLING BOOK

Published by
Bantam Doubleday Dell Books for Young Readers
a division of
Bantam Doubleday Dell Publishing Group, Inc.
1540 Broadway
New York, New York 10036

ISBN: 0-440-40495-9

Reprinted by arrangement with the author

Printed in the United States of America

August 1991

20 19 18 17 16 15 14 13 12

WES

To the wonderful metric system

without whose absence in this country

this book would not have been possible.

HOW BIG IS A FOOT?

Once upon a time
there lived a King
and his wife, the Queen.

They were a happy couple
for they had everything in the World.

However . . .

when the Queen's birthday came near

the King had a problem:

What could he give to Someone

who had Everything?

The King thought

and he thought and he thought.

Until suddenly, he had an idea!

HE WOULD GIVE THE QUEEN A BED.

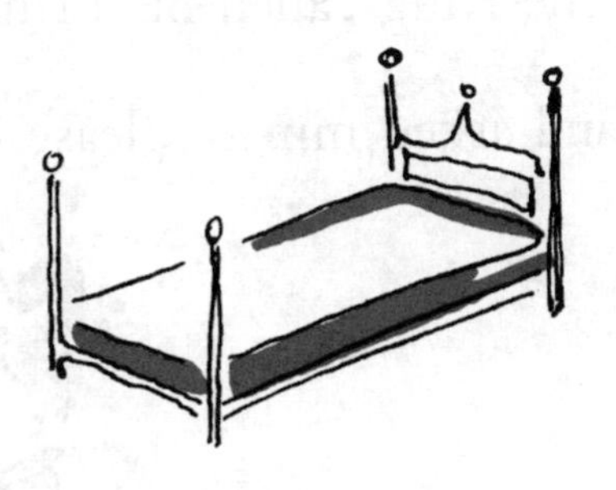

The Queen did not have a bed

because at the time

beds had not been invented.

So even Someone who had Everything—

did not have a bed.

The King called his Prime Minister

and asked him to please have a bed made.

The Prime Minister called the Chief Carpenter

and asked him to please have a bed made.

The Chief Carpenter called the apprentice

and told him to make a bed.

"How big is a bed?" asked the apprentice,

who didn't know because at the time

nobody had ever seen a bed.

"How big is a bed?"

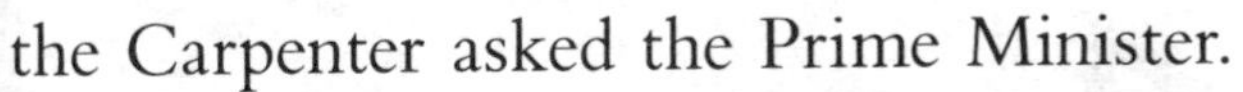

the Carpenter asked the Prime Minister.

"A good question," said the Prime Minister.

And he asked the King,

"HOW BIG *IS* A BED?"

The King thought and

he thought and he thought.

Until suddenly he had an idea!

THE BED

MUST BE BIG ENOUGH TO FIT THE QUEEN

The King called the Queen.

He told her to put on her new pajamas

and told her to lie on the floor.

The King took off his shoes

and with his big feet

walked carefully around the Queen.

He counted that

the bed must be

THREE FEET WIDE AND SIX FEET LONG

to be big enough to fit the Queen.

(Including the crown

which the Queen sometimes liked to wear to sleep.)

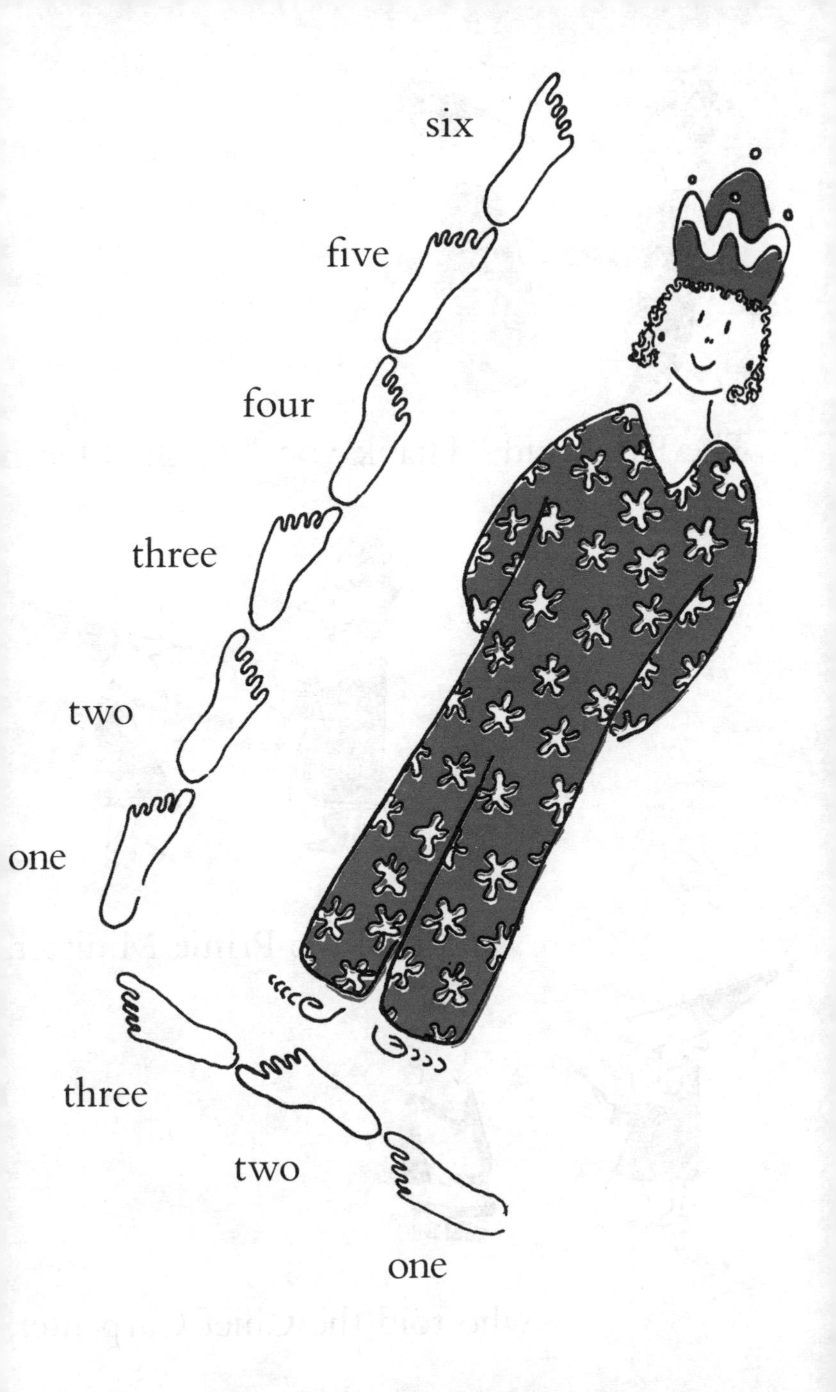
six
five
four
three
two
one
three
two
one

The King said "Thank you," to the Queen

and told the Prime Minister,

who told the Chief Carpenter,

who told the apprentice:

"The bed must be

three feet wide and six feet long

to be big enough to fit the Queen."

(Including the crown

which she sometimes liked to wear to sleep.)

The apprentice said "Thank you,"

and took off his shoes,

and with his little feet

he measured

six feet long

and

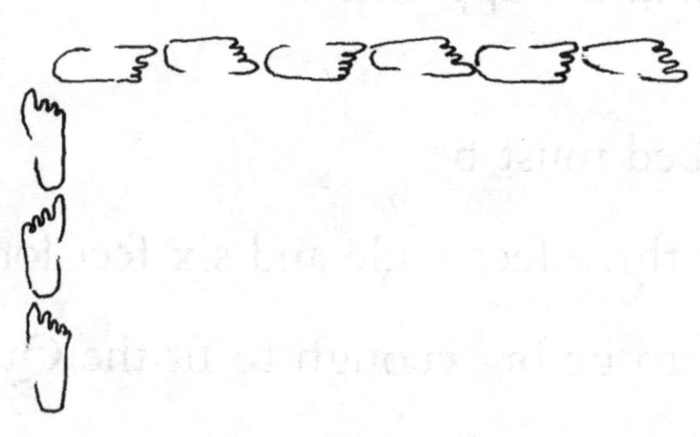

three feet wide

and made a bed to fit the Queen.

When the King saw the bed,

he thought it was beautiful.

He could not wait for the Queen's Birthday.

Instead, he called the Queen at once
and told her to put on her new pajamas.

Then he brought out the bed
and told the Queen to try it.

BUT

the bed was much too small for the Queen.

The King was so angry that he immediately

called the Prime Minister

who called the Chief Carpenter

who called the jailer

who threw the apprentice into jail.

The apprentice was unhappy.

WHY WAS THE BED
TOO SMALL FOR THE QUEEN?

He thought and

he thought and he thought.

Until suddenly he had an idea!

A bed that was three King's feet wide
and six King's feet long
was naturally bigger than
a bed that was three apprentice feet wide
and six apprentice feet long.

"I CAN MAKE A BED
TO FIT THE QUEEN
IF I KNOW THE SIZE
OF THE KING'S FOOT,"

he cried.

He explained this to the jailer,

who explained it to the Chief Carpenter,

who explained it to the Prime Minister,

who explained it to the King,

who was much too busy to go to the jai

Instead, the King took off one shoe

and called a famous sculptor.

The sculptor made an exact marble copy

of the King's foot.

This was sent to the jail.

The apprentice took the marble copy of the King's foot,

and with it he measured

three feet wide

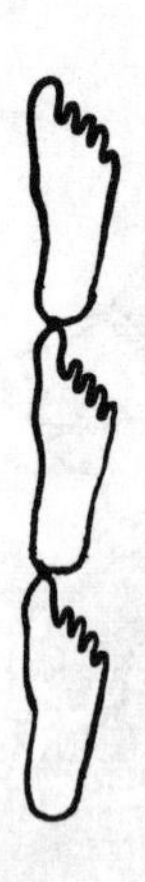

and six feet long

and built a bed to fit the Queen!

The Bed was ready just in time
for the Queen's Birthday.

The King called the Queen
and told her to put on her new pajamas.

Then he brought out the New Bed
and told the Queen to try it.

The Queen got into bed and . . .

THE BED FIT THE QUEEN PERFECTLY.

(Including the crown

which she sometimes liked

to wear to sleep.)

It was, without a doubt, the nicest gift that the Queen had ever received.

The King was very happy.

He immediately called the apprentice from jail and made him a royal prince.

He ordered a big parade, and all the people came out to cheer the little apprentice prince.

And forever after,

anyone who wanted to measure

anything

used a copy of the King's foot.

And when someone said,

"My bed is six feet long

and three feet wide,"

everyone knew exactly how big it was.